How the Birch Tree Got Its Stripes

A CREE STORY FOR CHILDREN

How the Birch Tree Got Its Stripes

A CREE STORY FOR CHILDREN

illustrated by George Littlechild
translated and edited by Freda Ahenakew

Fifth House
Saskatoon, Saskatchewan
1988

Canadian Cataloguing in Publication Data

Main entry under title:

How the birch tree got its stripes

   ISBN 0-920079-38-5

1. Cree Indians – Legends – Juvenile literature.
2. Indians of North America – Canada – Legends – Juvenile literature.
3. Legends – Canada – Juvenile literature.
4. Birch – Folklore – Juvenile literature.
I. Saskatchewan Indian Languages Institute.

E99.C88H69 1988   j398.2'08997   C88-098080-X

Special thanks to Freda Ahenakew for her invaluable assistance.

This book has been published with the assistance of:

Saskatchewan Arts Board
Canada Council

Published by

Fifth House Publishers
620 Duchess Street
Saskatoon, Saskatchewan
Canada S7K 0R1

Typeset by

Apex Graphics
Saskatoon, Saskatchewan

Printed in
Hong Kong by
Book Art Inc.
Toronto

Cover design: Robert Grey

Preface

This is a student story which was written in an intermediate Cree course at Saskatoon during the summer of 1982; we are grateful to Dean Whitstone for permission to edit and publish his work. This story was originally published in **kiskinahamawakan-acimowinisa / Student Stories** (Written by Cree-Speaking Students, Edited, Translated and with a Glossary by Freda Ahenakew, *Algonquian and Iroquoian Linguistics, Memoir 2,* Winnipeg 1986).

In the interest of the students who will work with the Cree version of the story, the writing has been standardized to represent the sounds of a single variant of Plains Cree — the central Saskatchewan dialect spoken on the **atahk-akohp** reserve.

This book has been prepared with the help and support of George Littlechild, who did the illustrations, and of Caroline Heath, who recognizes the need for publishing Cree legends for all children.

Since this is a traditional story, which is collectively owned by the Cree Indian people, the royalties from the sale of this book go to the Saskatchewan Indian Languages Institute.

One time Wisahkecahk had caught a lot of ducks.

Some of the ducks he plucked and some of them he put away.

Then Wisahkecahk built a fire to cook the ducks he had plucked.

While the ducks were cooking, Wisahkecahk started to think.

He was hungry, but he wanted to see if he could go for a long time without eating.

So he went to see these two birch trees and asked them if they would

hold him fast and not let him go right away, even if he was hungry.

The birch trees agreed to do what Wisahkecahk asked.

The birch trees held Wisahkecahk for a very long time.

Suddenly, a whiskey jack appeared.

He saw Wisahkecahk being held fast

and, oh my, he smelled the ducks cooking.

When Wisahkecahk saw the whiskey jack going to the place where his ducks were cooking, he yelled,

"Don't you touch my ducks!"

But the whiskey jack knew, of course, that Wisahkecahk couldn't do a thing. So off he flew.

In a little while the whiskey jack came back

with many other birds and animals.

Wisahkecahk was really angry.

He told the birches to let him go, but they wouldn't do it.

Wisahkecahk tried very hard to get loose

but he couldn't.

Finally, he fell asleep.

By the time Wisahkecahk woke up, the birds and animals had eaten all his ducks.

There was nothing left except a few feathers.

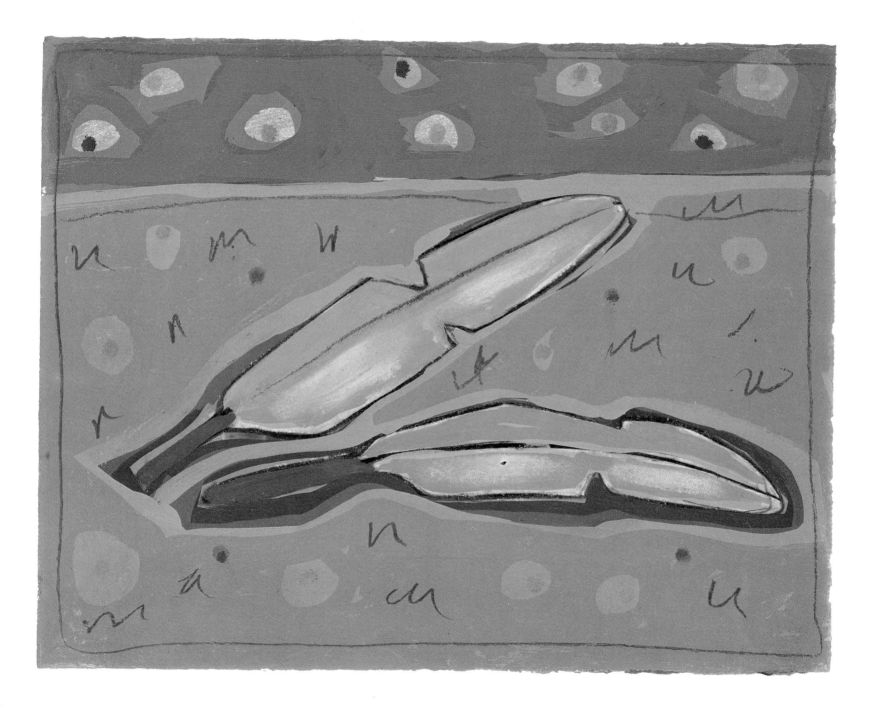

Finally the birches let Wisahkecahk go.

He went to the place where he had been doing his cooking—and found no ducks.

Wisahkecahk was so angry

he broke off some willow branches and gave the birches a real whipping.

And that's why, to this day, the birch trees are striped.